!N W!NTERT!ME

～BY～
KIM HOWARD

LOTHROP, LEE & SHEPARD BOOKS   NEW YORK

GLOSSARY

Fredag: Friday
(FRAY-dahg)

kjempe koseli: "giant cozy"
(SHEM-pah KOH-suh-lee)

morfar: grandfather [mother's father]
(moor-FAR)

mormor: grandmother [mother's mother]
(moor-moor)

rømme grøt: sour cream pudding
(ROHM-uh grüt)

ryggsekk: backpack
(RIG-uh-sehk)

sov godt: sleep well
(SOH-vuh goht)

velkommen tilbake: welcome back
(vehl-KOH-men teel-BAH-kuh)

FOR CHARLIE

∽

Library of Congress Cataloging in Publication
Howard, Kim. In Wintertime / Kim Howard.
p.   cm. Summary: A grandmother tells about her life as a child in the Scandinavian winter
with her grandmother. ISBN 0-688-11378-8.—ISBN 0-688-11379-6 (lib. bdg.) [1. Winter—
Fiction.   2. Grandmothers—Fiction.   3. Scandinavia—Fiction.]   I. Title. PZ7.H8322In
1994   [E]—dc20   93-108979 CIP AC

In wintertime, in my grandmother's house, we sit up late. I listen to her stories of a frozen land—the place where she was born, and her mother was born, and her grandmother was born. Her voice is cozy as she tells me:

In wintertime, the sun slept, and every day was dark and cold. Each morning Pappa lit the lamps while Mamma swept last night's snow from the porch. They spoke softly downstairs, thinking I was still asleep, but my eyes were wide open. I only wanted to stay warm as long as I could.

When the door closed behind Pappa, Mamma called me to get up. I opened my big blue shutters and shook my comforter till the feathers were fluffy again.

Then I ran downstairs for breakfast: warm rolls and
brown goat cheese, reindeer sausage from the farm, and
coffee with milk, even for me. The tablecloth was fresh
and white, like winter, and on it the candles were lit.

In winter, time was long, like the dark. Only the clock chimes told us it was time to go to market. Mamma laced my boots high to keep my feet dry while I pushed the sled. She picked up two baskets ready by the door and handed me a third. Then out into the cold we went. Her pockets jingled like ice, full of knitting things and coins and buttons.

Past Kira's and Jacob's and Liv's houses, along the edge of the fjord, we flew into our little town. Bright yellow boats groaned in the harbor, heavy with the weight of their catches, their engines still running to keep their men warm. Large, silent fishermen with carved stone faces stood on their decks with shrimp in their pails. By noon they'd have sold a whole night's work.

Even with mittens, our hands were tingling, but the crowd in the market would soon warm us up. Everyone there was a face I knew. Some hid behind steam of coffee and chocolate. Some hid between crates of oranges and fish. Some hid in their *ryggsekkene,* pulling out buttons to pay for their cheese.

Red-cheeked faces of chattering mammas hid behind needles that clittered and clattered. Wrinkly-faced grandpas hid behind pipe smoke, swapping their stories as they played checkers. Bright-bundled children moved too fast to hide.

In wintertime, *Fredag* was Mormor's day. We bought more apples and oranges than we did on other days, and tulips and lace and ribbon and fabric to take to the farm in the mountains. Our baskets were full when we left the market with presents for Mormor *and* Pappa's lunch.

There they sat, all our pappas, out there on the ice, huddled around a fire, fishing through a hole. From shore they looked as small as birds in the sky. We waved at them and they waved back. Then they edged across the ice to meet us, one boot in front of the other, not too much weight on either foot.

Mamma bit her lip every time, but Pappa knew what he was doing; he knew the ice. When he picked me up, his frosty whiskers stung my face. I buried my nose in his smoky coat. Mamma wrapped us both in sheepskin to take off the chill while we ate our lunch.

Before we had finished, the train whistle blew. No time today to show off my new skating turn or feed the geese any crumbs. Just time to pack our food and call good-byes. The train didn't wait on *Fredag*.

I loved that train, winding up and down, right then left, zigging and zagging across the glacier. I counted every train stop, every bridge and tunnel, every frozen waterfall along the way.

The twelfth stop was our stop. The train let out a long, low whistle, then pulled up to the platform with a hiss. Mamma and Pappa and I got off, and then the train was gone.

All around us was the forest, cold and very dark. And then a lantern swayed, a tiny welcome through the trees. Morfar had heard the whistle and come out to light our way.

We set off up the tiny path toward the light. Morfar's lantern grew brighter and brighter till I could see Mormor framed in the window.

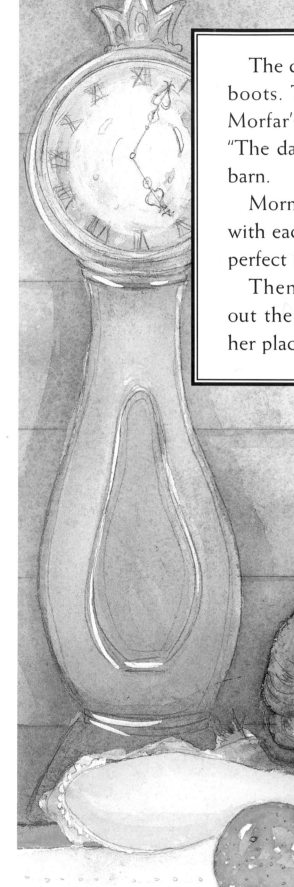

The door burst open. *"Velkommen tilbake!"* Off with our boots. Then Mormor's hugs were all around us, and Morfar's eyes were happy even though he grumbled, "The day's too short," as he and Pappa headed for the barn.

Mormor unwrapped our bundles, hugging us again with each one. "Look at these oranges! The lace will be perfect for Kristin's collar!"

Then Mamma stirred soup while Mormor spread out the fancy tablecloth and I stacked soup bowls at her place.

Just as we lit the candles, Pappa and Morfar came in, knowing that supper was ready without being told.

Morfar said a thankful prayer. Then Mormor ladled out the soup and Mamma brought on the plate of trout and I carried in a bowl of tender potatoes.

The steam from our soup warmed our faces and the bowls warmed our hands as we ate and chattered. There was a whole week to tell about.

When supper was over, Pappa stepped outside to light the snowball lamps on the path. Morfar went to his chair to smoke his pipe. Mamma made waffles while I cleared the table and Mormor filled it again with almond cakes and stuffed apples, bowls of rice pudding, glogg, and elderberry juice.

Then the door creaked open and the wind blew in and with it came Aunt Vesla, Uncle Knut, Aunt Gertrude and Uncle Erik, and Tor and Anna.

"*Kjempe koseli!*" they said, and they were right, it *was* cozy.

Uncle Erik sat at the organ, and Uncle Knut put his violin under his chin. Aunt Gertrude and Aunt Vesla gathered up their skirts, and the music began. Our heels clicked and our toes tapped on the polished floor and we laughed and sang and danced until we couldn't anymore.

Pappa opened the door for the winter night to cool us off. Then we surrounded the table to fill our plates with sweets.

Uncle Erik always sat next to the almond cakes and nearly ate them all. Tor cracked nuts loudly and Anna stood over the *rømme grøt,* searching for surprises inside: A ring meant marriage, an almond meant good luck, and a penny was for wealth. Mamma found the ring and grabbed Uncle Knut's arm, winking at Pappa, who never noticed.

Then Uncle Erik muttered that the moon was high, though there wasn't a moon, and Uncle Knut packed up his violin carefully. All the aunts and uncles and cousins bundled up again.

"*Sov godt*," they said. I watched them disappear into the forest through a curtain of snow crystals gathered on the window.

In the open cupboard where my bed was made, my treasures were safe on the window ledge: dried butterflies from summer, lacy reindeer moss from spring, a bird's nest I found when the trees lost their leaves in autumn.

Hidden in my cupboard bed, I snuggled under the blanket and listened to the soft talk of Mamma and Morfar cleaning up. I wanted to lie there and look outside at the dark night, but my pillow was too deep to see over.

I knew that Pappa had blown out all the lamps and Mormor was in bed knitting, waiting up for Morfar, who had gone back out to the barn. I knew that Mamma and Pappa would wake me in the morning before anyone else was moving. I was warm and the bed was soft. It was time now to sleep.

My grandmother's eyes close and her knitting falls.
I watch her sleep. I know she is dreaming of another
story in wintertime....